# GRILLED CHEESE MURDER

## THE DARLING DELI SERIES, BOOK 4

PATTI BENNING

SUMMER PRESCOTT BOOKS PUBLISHING

# CHAPTER ONE

"Candice, can you grab the mop again?" Moira Darling called out to her daughter. The blond twenty-year-old poked her head out of the kitchen, took one look at the puddle of dirty water on the deli's floor, and ducked back through the swinging door, to emerge a few seconds later with a mop and bucket in hand.

Moira was glad that the weather had finally broken; a late spring was better than none at all. However, the warm weather came with its own set of problems, namely the seemingly endless amounts of muddy slush tracked in on people's boots. The weatherman had announced just this morning that another cold front was moving towards them, which meant that in a few days all of the snow melt would turn back into slick, deadly ice.

For now, though, the warmer weather was encouraging people to leave their houses and come to town to stock up on goods before bad weather returned. Darling's DELIcious Delights had been bustling with familiar faces today. It was, in fact, the busiest that the store had been since the crowds of tourists that the Winter Festival had brought in a few weeks before.

"I think I'll just leave this out here," Candice said after she had finished cleaning up the muddy puddle that had been left by their latest customer. "I'm sure we'll need it again soon."

"Good idea," Moira replied. "How's the soup of the day holding up?" In honor of the nice weather, she had made her famous spring onion soup. Always a favorite, it seemed especially popular today. The light yet flavorful broth combined with rice noodles and chopped green onions was a dramatic change from the heavier soups and thick, savory stews that she usually made during the winter.

"We've still got about a third of the broth left. I just put some noodles in the smaller pot for us," her daughter replied. The rice noodles cooked quickly, taking just a few minutes to reach the perfect al dente state. To keep them from getting soggy, Moira had to cook each batch separately as the customer ordered it.

"Great, I'm starving," she said. "I'll go make us a couple of bowls of salad in a few minutes, if you'll watch the register."

"It's a deal." Candice joined her mother behind the counter, leaning casually against the refrigerated glass case. "What are you working on?"

"Oh, I'm just going through some of the deli's financial records. I'm comparing our bank statements with the ones from this time last year... we're making almost twice what we were," she said happily.

The deli had started out as a hobby for Moira a few years ago, but it had quickly grown into a thriving business. With her shelves full of organic cold cut meats, artisan cheeses from local Amish farms, and a variety of products from local farms and businesses, her store was unique in the area. The people of Maple Creek seemed to like knowing that they were supporting their local economy when they shopped there, and summer tourists couldn't get enough of the quality food that she sold. The deli also served a daily soup and sandwich or soup and salad combo, which was Moira's personal favorite aspect of the little shop. She enjoyed coming up with new recipes, and loved seeing people enjoy the food that she created.

"That's amazing," her daughter said. "I've been reading so many stories of small businesses failing lately that I've been getting worried about whether or not I'll be able to keep a candy shop running. I guess I just have to remember that for every failed business, there's also a success story like yours."

"I think you'll do great, sweetie," she told the young woman. "You know more than I did when I started out, and you've got my support and the support of everyone that works here. And I'm sure your boyfriend will be a big help too; he seems like a smart young man. How is Adrian, anyway?"

"Oh, he's fine. He does want to help me with the candy shop, but I'm not sure I want to keep dating him. We might just end up as business partners instead." Candice shrugged. "He is really good at figuring out how much everything will cost though. He's already saving me the cost of an accountant. How are you and David doing?" Her daughter gave her a sly look, referring to David Morris, the private investigator who had helped them out of some recent sticky situations.

"There is no me and David, we're just friends,"

Moira said, half amused and half irritated. "But he's doing well, from what I've heard."

"You can't be *that* blind, Mom. You've got to know that he likes you as more than 'just friends.' He wouldn't hang around and help out at the deli so much if he didn't."

"He's just being friendly—you'll understand when you're our age. Oh, speaking of David, he said that he knew someone who's thinking of closing down his business and moving out of Lake Marion. His store is right on Main Street, so it would be perfect for you. Do you want to go take a look at it?" Moira attempted to change the subject. She was relieved when it worked; the truth was, she *did* have feelings beyond friendship for the private detective that had helped her so much recently, but she didn't know if he thought of her as anything more than a good friend and she wasn't willing to risk their friendship to find out.

Candice jumped on the distraction. "Right on Main Street? That sounds perfect. How big is the display window? Do you know if he's planning on leasing the building or selling it? Does it have a natural gas hookup?"

"Slow down, slow down," Moira said with a chuckle. "I don't know much, but he said that we can come and look at it today or tomorrow if you want."

"Can we go today? As soon as we close the deli?"

Unable to resist Candice's eager face, the deli owner agreed. "As long as the temperature doesn't drop. I don't want to be driving on icy roads if I can help it. Just don't get your hopes too high," she warned. "David said his friend wasn't even a hundred percent sure he was going to sell it. I'll call him and ask if he can meet us there."

"I know, I'll try to keep my expectations realistic, but

—" Candice was cut off when the deli's front door swung open. A young man walked in. His olive skin and gray eyes looked familiar, but Moira couldn't quite place his face.

"Welcome to Darling's DELIcious Delights," she said brightly. "Feel free to take a look around. Our Soup of the Day is Spring Onion, and that comes with an Asian ginger salad."

"I'll take a bowl of the soup," he said. "No salad. And can you do that to go?"

"Sure thing." As her daughter ducked into the kitchen to get the young man a bowl of soup, Moira rang the order up. "Will you be paying with cash or card?" she asked. He looked up from the wall of photos he'd been examining. The photos were all of local people, plus a few pictures of the winning ice sculptures from the Winter Festival. A group shot of everyone that worked at the deli had the place of honor in the center. Darrin, one of her young clerks, had thought up the photo display, and the locals loved it.

"Oh, um, cash." He reached into his pocket and brought out a few crumpled ones, which he placed on the counter near the register. When Candice came back out with his order, he mumbled a thanks and left. Moira stared after him for a few seconds, certain that she had seen him before. *Maybe he's related to someone I know*, she thought. Then she shrugged and left Candice to handle the young woman that had just walked in, while she whipped up some salads and a couple of bowls of soup to serve as a quick lunch for the two of them.

# CHAPTER TWO

Luckily for them the weather held, so after the two of them closed up the deli for the evening, they headed down the road to Lake Marion. It was a scenic drive, with thick forest abutting either side of the Michigan highway. As they got closer, they could begin to see the lake that the town was named after through the trees. Late evening sunlight glinted off the patchy ice that still covered the majority of the water's surface. It really was a beautiful town. Moira often wished that Maple Creek had a lake so close to town, but she supposed that the small river that ran through the park sufficed well enough.

David's car was already parked outside of the toy store that, if their luck held, would soon be repurposed into a candy shop for her daughter. She parked behind him and she and Candice walked inside together. The private investigator was talking to a woman at the counter, and Moira walked over to join him while her daughter took in the wide display window and pre-installed shelves.

"Hey," David said, smiling at her when she reached the counter. "How was the drive?"

"It was nice," she replied. "I can see why Candice wants to live here."

"Well once she moves, you'll have an excuse to visit whenever you want." He flashed her a quick grin, and then turned his attention back to the woman behind the counter. "Can you at least tell me where he is?" he asked her.

"Sorry, he asked me not to say," she replied. "I'll tell

you when he gets back if you leave me your number."

"He has it—like I said, we've been friends for years." David sighed. "Look, if you see him, can you just ask him to return my call? He sounded worried the last time I spoke with him, and I want to make sure he's all right."

"I will. You three can look around if you want. Everything's thirty percent off," she said.

He and Moira thanked the woman and headed across the store where Candice was taking pictures with her cell phone. "I'm hoping that Adrian will be able to get some sort of measurements from these," she told them. "This place looks perfect. I don't think I could even imagine a better building to set up my shop in."

"I'm glad you like it," David said. "As soon as my

friend gets back from wherever he took off to, I can try to get a price from him."

"How soon are they planning on selling it?" Moira asked, looking around at the toy shop. The shelves were still lined with stuffed animals, old-fashioned wooden toys, and shiny new electronics. It didn't have the look of a store that was going out of business.

"Henry—my friend—seemed like he wanted to find a buyer within a few months. But Alice, that's his granddaughter, the woman at the counter, didn't seem so sure. Sorry," he added, looking over at Candice. "He didn't tell me he was going to be out of town."

"That's fine, if he's not around to sell it right now, that means no one else will be able to snap it up before I get the funds together for a down payment." Candice grinned, looking around the small space with a gleam in her eye that reminded Moira of how she herself had felt when she had first seen the building that was to become her deli.

"I like your positive attitude," the private investigator said with a laugh. "Feel free to keep looking around for as long as you like. Why don't you leave your number with Alice so Henry can contact you when he gets back." He turned to Moira. "We can go wait outside and let her get a feel for the place on her own."

She followed David outside, glancing back only once to make sure her daughter was happy. She was glad to see that the young woman was still eagerly taking pictures of the store, her face bright and hopeful.

"I hope that this place works out for her," she said to David as the door shut behind them with a jingle. The air outside was chilly, but compared to the bitingly cold temperatures of just a few days ago, it was almost pleasant. Night had begun to fall, and streetlights lit up the small twilight town.

"Me too. I don't know where Henry could have gotten to—this really isn't like him." She saw worry flit across his face for a split second before he shook his head and offered her a small smile. "But that isn't what I wanted to talk to you about." He fell silent, and Moira raised an eyebrow, waiting for him to continue. Though not exactly talkative, the private investigator was rarely at a loss for words when something needed to be said.

"I was wondering," he began after a moment. "Would you like to go out to dinner with me?"

"Dinner sounds nice," she replied, slightly flustered. "Is this a... date?"

"If you want it to be," he said easily, "then yeah, it is."

"It's a date then." A grin tugged at the corners of her

lips. Candice had been right after all. She felt a small stirring of nerves in her belly. It had been far too long since she had dated anyone, let alone someone she liked as much as she liked David.

"What evening is best for you?" he asked.

"Oh, any night after we close the deli is fine. Your schedule is less predictable than mine, so you should just choose an evening that's convenient for you."

"Does this Wednesday night sound good? I can pick you up at half past eight," he offered.

"That's perfect." Wednesday was the day after tomorrow, which would give her some time to prepare. Did she even have anything she could wear on a date? "I'm looking forward to it."

## CHAPTER THREE

Her good mood lasted all night and well into the morning of the next day. Candice had given her a few quizzical glances on the way home, but Moira kept her upcoming date to herself, wanting to cherish the eager, hopeful feeling for as long as she could. While she loved her daughter, she knew that Candice would want to speculate about where a relationship with David might lead. The deli owner didn't want to think too much about the future right now—she wanted to focus on how perfect the present was. She would tell Candice about the date just before she went out with him, but for now it was her happy little secret.

On Tuesday, Dante was the only worker on staff and

as usual he haunted the back room, keeping tabs on the soup and restocking the front as needed. She had hired him only a few months ago and he had quickly proven himself reliable and trustworthy. In many ways, he was still a mystery to her. He had appeared seemingly out of the ether shortly after she began looking for a new employee and he seemed not to have any connections to the small town whatsoever. Yet he had never once let her down, not even after a murdered food critic had been found in the deli during the Winter Festival.

"Hey, Ms. Darling, is it all right if I take a quick lunch break?" he asked her shortly after noon.

"Go ahead," she told him. "I should be able to handle everything on my own for a while." *Maybe I spoke too soon*, she thought as a couple of cars pulled into the parking lot just as her employee disappeared behind the kitchen doors.

"Hi," she said to the first pair of customers to walk in.

It was a woman and her young daughter. They came in every few weeks. "Welcome to Darling's DELIcious Delights. Feel free to look around. Our Soup of the Day today is Red Pepper Asparagus, and it comes with grilled cheese on zucchini bread."

"Zucchini bread? Eww," the little girl asked, wrinkling her nose. The mother shushed her, shooting Moira an apologetic glance. The deli owner just laughed.

"If it's all right with your mom, I'll let you try a piece." The mother nodded, so she ducked into the kitchen to butter a slice of the tasty bread for the girl. When she came back out, a third customer had wandered in. He was a tall man, but thin, with scraggly blonde hair and a hungry look about him. She nodded to him, and then gave the piece of zucchini bread to the girl, who bit into it and smiled hugely.

After ringing up the mom and little girl, who ended

up each getting a bowl of soup with an extra order of grilled cheese on zucchini bread, she turned her attention to the man who was standing at the back.

"Can I help you?" she asked.

"I think I'll just look around," he replied. As he began slowly perusing the refrigerated cases, Moira sat back on her stool. She kept half an eye on him, but focused the rest of her attention on the order form she was working on. She couldn't wait until summer when the local farms would be practically overflowing with fresh produce. *Maybe I'll let one of them set up a fresh produce stand outside again,* she thought. Last summer, she had allowed a young woman to sell fresh black sweet cherries on the sidewalk in front of her store during farmer's market days. She recalled the sweet, rich flavor of the delicious fruit.

"I'm done with lunch, Ms. Darling. What can I-" Dante's voice cut off suddenly. Moira turned to see him poking his head out of the kitchen, his grey eye wide. She followed his gaze to see that he was staring at the tall man who was still examining the wares. Without a word, he slipped back into the kitchen. Worried and confused, she could do nothing but stare after her young employee. What was going on with him today?

A moment later the tall man left without buying anything and Moira got up to find Dante. He was busily scrubbing dishes at the wide sink in the kitchen. When she approached, he looked up and greeted her casually as if nothing out of the ordinary had happened.

"Did you want me to start thawing more zucchini bread, or do you think we have enough?" he asked her. She frowned for a second, not sure whether she should ask him about his odd reaction. With a mental shrug, she decided not to talk about it if he didn't want to. He had always been the most private of her employees, and it wasn't her place to push him for an explanation that he didn't want to give.

"I think we've got enough, but if you're concerned about it, feel free to take out one more loaf. You can always bring it home for dinner if we don't end up using it," she told him. "We have plenty of the stuff; I bought about twenty pounds of zucchini last year, and what I didn't make into soup, I made into bread and froze."

As she walked out of the kitchen, she did her best to push the incident out of her mind. It was a nice day, the sun was shining, and she had a date to look forward to tomorrow night.

# CHAPTER FOUR

"I can't believe that you didn't tell me." Candice bounced on the balls of her feet, her excitement overcoming any annoyance she might have felt for being out of the loop. Moira grinned at her, and then half turned, trying to look at herself in the mirror. She was wearing black slacks that somehow miraculously still fit her, even though they had been sitting in her closet for who knew how long, and a loose red blouse. Her hair was pulled up in a fancy sort of bun that Candice had managed to create in only a few minutes.

"I did tell you," she pointed out to her daughter. "I just waited a little bit. It's not like you tell me every time you go out on a date."

"True," the young woman replied. "But I go out on dates all the time. You go out so rarely that it should be considered a national holiday."

"Oh, hush," she told Candice fondly. "Just tell me if my outfit looks okay."

"You look great, Mom." They embraced, Moira feeling younger than her years and more excited than she had thought she would be. It wasn't like she hadn't gone out to eat with David before, but that had always been last minute and out of necessity when they were both hungry, or when he had stopped by for lunch at the deli. Going out together for a dinner that they both acknowledged was a date would be different. She only hoped that things weren't awkward between them. She cherished the easy friendship that they had built over the past few months.

"I think he's here," her daughter said a moment later, peering out the window. "You've got to tell me everything when you get back. And don't do anything I wouldn't do!"

She met David at the door, taking the arm that he offered her as she navigated the icy walkway. The temperature was dropping rapidly, and everything that had melted during the last few days was refreezing. She was glad that David would be driving instead of her, and doubly glad that they didn't have far to go. They pulled up at the Redwood Grill, the new restaurant that had opened in town not long ago. It was a gorgeous steakhouse that had amazing —if a bit pricey—food. Moira knew the owner personally. In fact, Denise stopped in at the deli a couple of times a week to chat with her. They were the only two female restaurant owners in town, and had formed a sort of automatic friendship. She was also sure that the lack of direct competition between their businesses helped them maintain that friendship.

"You look gorgeous," David told her as he opened

the passenger side door for her. They had both been unusually quiet on the car ride over, and Moira was beginning to envy her daughter's easy-going attitude when it came to dating. She really was pretty out of practice.

"Thanks," she said, smiling up at him. "You look pretty nice yourself." It was true, he had obviously put effort into his outfit. He usually dressed stylishly, openly favoring a clichéd private investigator look. Tonight, however, he was wearing a dress shirt and neatly pressed black pants. He smelled nice too, like soap and cologne.

"I hope it's all right that we came here," he added as they walked towards the restaurant's entranceway. "I know that you and Candice frequent this place, but it's the nicest place around and I didn't think it would be a good idea to drive too far with the roads like this."

"I love this place," she assured him. "I could eat here every night and not get tired of it."

The hostess seated them quickly, taking them back to the same booth that Moira and her daughter had sat in on the grill's opening night. It had become their regular table, and the hostess gave her a quick grin of recognition, raising a discreet eyebrow as she glanced at David. The deli owner felt a faint blush rise on her cheeks. She hadn't thought of the fact that since everyone who worked at the grill knew her, her date with the private investigator would soon be the talk of the town.

A few minutes later, the two of them were sipping wine and beginning to talk comfortably again. Moira was relieved that the awkwardness had faded quickly. She was still concerned about the date affecting their friendship, but at least they were having fun.

"Do you know if that guy from the toy store ever

contacted Candice?" she asked him once they had both put their menus down.

"No, as far as I know, he's still out of town." A frown flitted across David's face. "It's odd. I've known him for years, and he's always told me if he's planning on going on a trip. He does have a cabin up north, but I don't know why he wouldn't be returning my calls."

"Are you worried about him?"

"I am a little concerned," he admitted. "But his granddaughter keeps telling me that he's fine, so I guess there's nothing I can do."

"I hope everything is all right, both for them and for Candice. She really likes the place."

"I know." His face relaxed into a smile. "I don't think

he'll keep her waiting too much longer. How are all of the plans for the candy shop coming?"

"From what I've seen, she and Adrian have been making a ton of progress." She chuckled. "I have to admit; I don't understand half of what they're saying. I hired people to help me get the deli running, but those two are doing most of it by themselves."

"You must be proud of her," he said.

"Oh, I am. Proud and worried. I know she's smart and capable of running a store, but there's just so much that can go wrong, and she's going to be putting a lot of money into it." She took another sip of wine, and was casting around for something else to talk about when she felt her phone buzz in her pocket. Shooting David an apologetic glance, she pulled it out and glanced at the screen. When she saw the caller ID, she felt her blood turn to ice.

"Hello?" she said, pressing the phone to her ear.

"Ms. Darling, this is Trish at the Maple Creek Police Department. We need you to come down to the station for us as soon as possible."

"Why?" Moira said, her voice sounding hollow. David was gazing at her with concern in his blue eyes.

"There's been a death, and we need you to identify the body."

# CHAPTER FIVE

As David drove her to the police station, an uncomfortable silence once again fell over them. All Moira could do was keep repeating to herself, *It's not Candice, it's not Candice.* That had been the first thing out of her mouth to the woman from the police station. Her daughter was fine, which was the important thing, but the name that they had given her instead was nearly as bad. When they got there, she saw that the small building was busy for so late at night. Detective Jefferson met her and David at the door.

"Right this way," he said, leading them both back down familiar hallways to one of the more comfortable interview rooms. "Normally we wouldn't do this, but he had you as his emergency contact in his phone. We couldn't find any family to contact." The detective sighed and put a blue folder down on the coffee table in the center of the room. "I'm really sorry to ask this of you." He looked between the two of them. "Whenever you're ready." Moira took a deep breath, traded a glance with David, and then opened the folder.

"It's not him," she gasped, feeling relief course through her. "It's not Dante." Horror was close on the heels of her relief though, as the grisly scene in the photos registered in her brain. The body was someone that she recognized, but thankfully not someone that she knew. Instead of Dante's familiar face, she saw the empty gaze of the young man that had come into the store a few days ago, the one who had seemed so familiar at the time. The similarities between him and Dante were now obvious, and she couldn't believe that she hadn't made the connection before. Trying to ignore the bloodstained carpet under the boy in the photo, she handed it over to David so he could get a closer look.

"What happened?" she asked, turning back to Jefferson. "Where's Dante?"

"If that's not him, then we don't know. But it doesn't look good," he said grimly. "We got a call from Dante's neighbor earlier today, a complaint about a gunshot. When we got there, we found him." He nodded at the blue folder in David's hands. "He matched the description of the resident, so we thought it must be Dante. But if you're sure that it isn't, well, that means we have more questions than before, and fewer answers."

"This is so terrible. Do you think that there's any chance that Dante's okay?" she asked.

"I honestly don't know what to tell you, Ms. Darling. We don't know what's going on here, and we don't know yet whether we should be considering Dante to be a possible victim, or a suspect." He rubbed his hand across his face, looking weary. "Anything you can tell us about him will be helpful. We don't have much to go on right now. How long has he worked for you?"

"Just a few months, " Moira said. He had worked for her since shortly after she'd lost another employee . "I'm sorry to say I don't really know him that well. He's a very private person, but I never got the feeling that he was dangerous. He's been nothing but helpful at the deli, and I've been able to rely on him to show up on time and put a hundred and one percent into his work."

"Do you know where he moved here from?" the detective asked.

"No, I don't," she admitted. "Sorry."

"It's all right," he told her. "We're just trying to get a feel for him right now. Do you know of any family or friends that he might have been in contact with?"

"Other than my other employees, whom he was friendly with, no," she said. "Like I said, he was a private guy."

"All right. If you do think of anything else, don't hesitate to give me a call." He stood up and gave her a sympathetic grimace. "It's getting late, so I'll let you two get going. If you hear from Dante, or see him, please let me know immediately."

"I will," she promised.

Still feeling shaky, she got up and followed the detective back down the hallway. David trailed behind them, handing the blue folder back to the detective before gently guiding Moira out of the police station and into the chilly car.

"I'll take you home," he said as he started the engine. "I'm sorry about Dante. I hope he's all right."

"Me too. I'm really worried about him." She hesitated. "What do you think happened?"

"Well, if I didn't know him—and you—I'd say that it looks like he killed that boy and then took off."

"But you do know him," she pointed out. "You don't really think that he would do that... do you?"

"I don't know what to think," he said. "You can see what things look like, Moira. What do you think happened? That the other guy showed up at Dante's apartment and then shot himself in the chest?" Remembering the gruesome image in the blue folder, the deli owner shuddered.

"Well, no," she said. "I know that isn't very likely. But even if Dante *did* shoot him, couldn't it have been in self-defense? What if the guy attacked him?"

"If he was justified in shooting him, then why would he run?" David asked.

"Because he's probably *scared*," Moira said quietly. "He's just a kid. He doesn't have any family in town. I mean, he put *me* as his emergency contact. He obviously doesn't have anyone he can go to for help."

"Maybe you're right," the private investigator said. "I'm not saying I'm convinced that he murdered that guy, but we have to be prepared for the possibility that he's guilty." He paused, keeping his eyes on the road. "There is another possibility, you know."

"What?" she asked, feeling ill. She wasn't sure that she wanted to hear more.

"What if there was a third person there? Maybe this third person and the dead guy were working together, maybe not, but I can't imagine that it bodes well for Dante either way. This could be a kidnapping gone wrong, or maybe some sort of old family feud. I think you should prepare yourself for the possibility that he might not be alive," he said.

Moira was silent, at a loss for what to say. When she had gotten the phone call earlier at the restaurant, she had gone into the police station expecting to identify her employee's body. The relief that she had felt when it wasn't had been unparalleled. She didn't want to think that the next time she went in, it might actually be him.

"I don't want to just give up on him," she said at last. They were driving slowly through town, the orange streetlights reflecting off of the icy sidewalks. Something occurred to her. "Did Detective Jefferson say anything about whether Dante's car was still in the parking lot?" she asked. "If it is, then that might mean that he has been kidnapped and maybe they could put out some sort of alert."

"I don't think he said anything about it," he told her.

"But even if his car is there, he could have fled on foot. Or if he was working with someone, they might have given him a ride."

"Can we go check?" she asked, convinced that seeing the scene of the crime would help her put things together. "We could just drive through the parking lot. I know what his car looks like. The apartment complex is only a few minutes away."

"All right," David agreed, giving her a quick, unreadable look. "We'll just drive through and see if the car is there. But after that, I think we should just let the police do their jobs. And you should keep an eye out for him. You're one of the few people that he knows in town; if he needs help, he'll likely try to contact you, Candice, or Darrin. And just keep in mind, we don't know yet whether he is guilty or innocent."

# CHAPTER SIX

They drove through the parking lot twice, and Moira kept her eyes peeled for her employee's car. She saw it parked in the deli's lot most days, and was certain that she wouldn't have trouble spotting it if it was there. She didn't know whether the fact that the car was gone was good or bad. She supposed that it meant it was more likely that Dante was alive, but it also made it seem more likely that he was guilty of killing the young man who had been shot in his apartment.

"Thanks," she said to David when they pulled into her driveway. It was late, but her mind was racing too quickly for her to feel very tired. "And I'm sorry that our date ended the way that it did."

"We can try it again sometime," he said, giving her a quick smile to reassure her that he wasn't upset. "After we find your missing employee." A light in her house flickered on, and Moira knew that it meant that her daughter was still up, waiting to hear a report of the date. She wasn't looking forward to the ensuing conversation; Candice would be worried about Dante, and would ask her mother many questions that she just didn't have the answers to.

"I really hope he's okay." She sighed. "I'd better go in and get this over with."

"Good luck. Do you want me to stop by the deli tomorrow? I'll see if I can dig anything up on Dante, or at least get some leads as to who the dead guy is," he offered.

"Sure." Despite herself, she found a small smile tugging at the corners of her lips. Somehow David still wanted to be around her, even though trouble seemed to follow her like a hungry dog. "See you tomorrow."

She let herself out of the car and walked the short distance to her porch. As soon as her foot touched the first step to the porch, her front door opened and Candice stood silhouetted against the warm glow from inside. She rushed her mother inside, her eyes gleaming as she eagerly waited to hear Moira's story of the date. Her expectant expression faded slowly as she got a better look at her mother's face.

"Oh, no," she said. "What happened?"

Moira told her daughter the story over a mug of hot chocolate. Her brightly painted kitchen seemed far too cheery for such a grim tale. She was purposely vague when she described the photograph, not wanting to have to go into grisly detail.

"I don't even know what to say," Candice said when she was done. "I mean, I'm glad that Dante isn't the one who got shot, but... it's almost worse if he's the one that killed the other guy, you know?"

"Do you really think that Dante would murder someone?" she asked her daughter. She had been trying to assume the best of her missing employee, but both David and her daughter seemed ready to throw him under the bus, so to speak.

"Not really, but neither of us has been too great at spotting killers recently," the young woman said pointedly. Moira frowned, hurt. She'd met several killers in the past few months and hated remembering their crimes; she hadn't ever felt so betrayed by anyone before, not even when she had found out that her husband was cheating on her. She didn't want to let the experience damage her trust in people's good nature, but maybe her daughter and David had a point. Most of the time, the simplest solution was the right one. When you start out with two young men, and one is found dead and the other is missing, there was only one probable answer.

"Did he ever tell you anything about where he came from, or his family or anything?" Moira asked, trying to leave the subject of Dante's innocence or guilt. Either way, what was important right then was finding him.

"I don't think so..." her daughter trailed off, biting her lower lip as she thought back. "I asked him once why he moved to Maple Creek, and he just said because he liked the town, and he didn't really have anywhere else to go. I didn't pry."

"I never pushed him for answers either, but now I wish I did." She sighed. "Apparently the police don't even have any information about where he's from or where his family is. Did you ever meet any of his friends?"

"Besides me and Darrin, he never really seemed to hang out with anybody," her daughter said. "He seemed pretty used to just doing his own thing."

"The poor young man." Moira frowned. "It must be terrible not to have anyone to rely on."

"He relied on you," Candice pointed out. "You told me that the police said that he put you as his emergency contact in his cell phone. He must have known that you would do what it took to help him if he was ever in an accident or something. Maybe he'll come to you if he needs help."

"I hope so. As long as he isn't a danger to you—or me—then I'd be happy to help him however I can. Will you let me know if you hear from him?" she asked her daughter.

"Of course," the young woman agreed. "Are you going to tell Darrin what's going on?"

GRILLED CHEESE MURDER

"I think I need to," she replied after thinking about it for a moment. "He and Dante are pretty close, and he should know that his friend's in trouble. Plus, word gets around this town quickly and I think it's better if he hears it from us than from the news." She closed her eyes, her hands cupped around the warm mug. She was beginning to feel tired, and it was looking like she would have a lot to do tomorrow.

# CHAPTER SEVEN

Darrin came in early to work while she was dicing onions for the creamy spinach and orzo soup that would be the soup of the day. She took a moment to dump the onions in the pot, and then turned to greet him.

"Thanks for coming in so early," she said. "You might want to take a seat, there's something I need to tell you..."

His reaction, once he got past the initial shock, was similar to Candice's, though he sided with Moira when it came to the subject of whether or not he thought Dante had murdered the young man who looked so like him.

"He just doesn't seem the type," he said. "I mean, obviously, anyone can be the type, but Dante... is so easygoing. Why would he want to kill someone? It just doesn't seem like something he'd do."

"I'm glad *you* at least agree with me," Moira said. "I just wish Candice and David did also. When's the last time you heard from him?"

"A couple of days ago, when he called the deli to double-check his schedule for the week," her employee told her. "He sounded totally normal, and we made plans to hang out this weekend."

"Will you let me know if you hear from him again?" she asked. "I don't even know if he's still around, but if he is he might try to find one of us. Candice thinks we're pretty much the only people he knows in town."

"Yeah, no problem. I hope he turns up and everything ends up being fine. I like the guy."

"Me too," Moira said. "I just wish I felt like I could trust my judgment."

———

She was relieved when none of her customers mentioned anything about Dante. It seemed that the news of his mysterious disappearance hadn't yet been spread beyond the police station. She didn't know how many more crimes her little deli could be associated with and still stay in business.

While she served soup, made sandwiches, and rang up orders, she kept a careful eye on the street outside. She realized that she was half expecting to see Dante's car drive by. She didn't know what she'd do if she *did* see it. Run outside and chase it down? It ended up not mattering; she didn't so much as glimpse a car of the same make as his.

David came in shortly before the dinner rush. He had his leather bag with him, and waited until the deli was empty to set it on the glass counter and pull out a manila folder.

"I found some interesting stuff about our missing friend," he told her. "Remember how I told you I was going to run a background check on him a couple of months ago?" he asked. She nodded. "Well, the basic check didn't really turn much up. And by that, I mean there just wasn't much on it. At all. No employment history, no nothing. So, I had my guy dig a little deeper, and then forgot to check up on his progress once things started to get chaotic again." He handed her the folder. "Go ahead and take a look. Let me know if anything jogs your memory."

Feeling a bit guilty at the thought of reading secrets

that Dante wouldn't have wanted her to know, Moira took a seat on the stool behind the register and began reading. The files mentioned a town that Dante had never mentioned, but the picture that was attached was definitely his. There were records of the high school that he had graduated from, and the phone number of a diner that he had worked for. Moira frowned and handed the folder back to David.

"He never talked about any of that," she told David. "How did you find all of this?"

"My guy did a search using his first name and date of birth. What's really odd is that he had a different last name up until about a year ago," he told her. "I'm still looking into it. It's like one day he changed his name, got a different social security number, packed his bags, and left his hometown."

"Do you think he'll go back there?" she asked. "If that's where his family is, maybe he's going to them for help."

"He lived in a foster home, actually," he said. "From age ten onward. I still haven't found anything out about his birth parents."

"This keeps getting stranger and stranger." She tapped her fingers on the counter, thinking. "It's like he was running from something."

"And whatever he was running from caught up with him," said David in a grim voice.

CHAPTER EIGHT

David stayed at the deli, helping out for the last few hours before close. Moira was glad to find that they could work side by side without awkwardness, despite the fact that they had gone on a date and had yet to really talk about any feelings that they had for each other. She sent Darrin home early, with strict instructions to keep an eye out for his missing friend.

"So," she said to David once Darrin had cleared out. "Where should we start looking?"

"We aren't," he said, shaking his head. "It's too dangerous. He may have killed someone, and even if he didn't, there is someone else out there who *did*, and who is also likely going to be looking for him."

"That's all the more reason why we need to find him first," she pointed out. "To offer him help before whatever he's running from catches up to him."

"You shouldn't get yourself involved with this anymore than you already are," he told her. Then he added quietly, "I don't want to see you get hurt."

"I can't just stand around and do nothing when I know that someone I care about is in danger," she said. She was touched by his concern, but she knew that she wouldn't be able to live with herself if Dante got hurt and she didn't do everything she could to try to help him. David sighed.

"Fine, but I'm coming with you. I don't want you out there looking for him alone."

"It's a deal," she said with a grin. "That brings me back to my earlier question—where should we start looking for him?"

"Probably at his apartment," he said. "I don't know if we'll be able to get into his actual unit, but we can look around and ask people if they remember seeing anything out of the usual. If they have video cameras, I may be able to talk one of the security guys into letting us see the tape. You might recognize someone. It seems like half the town comes through the deli on a daily basis."

She was tempted to close early so that they could go investigate sooner, but she couldn't really justify it, not with the steady stream of customers that had been coming in all day. It wasn't until the ladle for the spinach orzo soup was coming up dry that she finally called it a day. Her stomach gave a hungry growl as she began rinsing out the pot. It was a pity that all the soup was gone—the rich, creamy flavor would have served well to warm her and David against the chilly night.

"Ready?" he asked when she came out of the kitchen.

"Yes," she responded. "Let's go."

"You checked the side door?" he asked, giving her a quick grin to show that he was half joking. Recently, someone had fixed the side door that they usually used for deliveries so that it couldn't latch shut, and had used it to sneak in without her knowledge. She had been terrified when she had discovered it, but thanks to David she now had surveillance in the deli in the form of a video camera and a motion detector. She had also added double-checking the door into her daily closing routine.

"You know it," she replied, surprised to find herself in such a good mood even though it had been such a grim twenty-four hours. She supposed that David just had the effect of making her feel safe. There was no one she would rather be spending the evening with.

"We can take my car. The roads are still icy, and it handles better in this sort of weather than yours does." He held the door for her on the way out, and then waited while she locked the deli up. If only Dante weren't missing and in trouble, the moment would have been perfect. She realized just how nice it was to have someone to spend time with. She had been far too solitary over the last few years.

## CHAPTER NINE

It was twilight by the time they reached Dante's apartment complex. Another quick sweep of the parking lot showed them that his car still wasn't there, so they parked in front of his building and got out. If she remembered correctly, his apartment was on the second floor.

"So, should we just go up?" she asked David. "Or should we go to the office or something first?"

"Let's just see what we can see for now," he suggested. "I doubt management would be much help at this point. Maybe we can stop in on our way out of here, if they're still open."

As they approached the building, Moira kept her eyes peeled for signs of anything out of place. She didn't see any security cameras, which was disappointing, though she knew that realistically she and David probably wouldn't have noticed anything that the police hadn't. The hallways of the apartment building smelled of stale cigarette smoke and some sort of industrial lemon-scented cleaner. The murmur of voices, possibly from a TV, came from behind one of the doors on the ground floor. The carpeting had stains on it, and one of the mailboxes was missing a door. She shuddered at the thought of Dante living in such a place. He was such a smart, hard-working young man. What must he have been running from to end up in a place like this?

Once they made their way up to the second floor, his apartment wasn't hard to find, as there was still torn crime scene tape across the door. It didn't take her long to see that there was nothing in the hallway that would be of any help to them.

"What now?" she asked, feeling oddly let down. What had she been expecting? To find Dante himself waiting for them?

"We could try talking to the neighbors if you want," David said. "Just keep in mind that they don't have to tell us anything."

"I think it's worth a shot." Before she lost her courage, she walked over and knocked on the door across the hall from Dante's. An older man with a yappy little dog in his arms answered. He gave the pair of them a questioning look.

"Hi," Moira said. "I hope we're not bothering you, but I'd love it if we could ask you a couple of questions about your neighbor, Dante."

"Who are you?" the man asked gruffly. "How do you know the kid?"

"David Morris, PI," David said, cutting in and flashing his identification to the man. "We're just trying to find him, and find out what's going on. This is Moira Darling, his employer." The man eyed them warily for a moment, and then seemed to come to a decision.

"All right, then," he said. "My name's Harrison. I'm the one that called the cops when I heard a gunshot. They didn't believe me at first, not until I told them I'm ex-military and definitely know what a gun sounds like." He snorted. "You'd think someone would come running when you say the word 'gunshot.' I guess that's not how things work these days."

"Did you see anything after you heard the gunshot?" Moira asked him, darting a glance towards the peephole in his door.

"No, the last tenant painted over the peephole," he explained, following her glance. "And I'm not going to open my door and stick my head out into the hallway when someone's shooting."

"Oh." She sighed. She had hoped for a second that it would be as easy as getting a blow-by-blow description of the events from Harrison, but she supposed that that would have been too easy. If he had seen anything, he would have already told the police, and from what Detective Jefferson had told her, they had no idea what had happened.

"How well did you know Dante?" David asked.

"He'd say hi to me if we passed each other in the hallway, but that's about it." The old man shrugged. "There's not much to say about him. He's quiet, kept to himself. He never had parties or anything, never even had anyone over that I noticed."

"Did you hear anything besides a gunshot the evening that the young man was killed?"

"No," the man replied. Then he frowned. "Well, come to think of it, yes. I heard a few people talking or arguing a few minutes before, but they could have come from anyone on this floor. Someone slammed a door also."

"A few? So more than just two? Did you tell the police this?" Moira asked.

"I didn't think of it then. Someone had just been shot, and everything was so chaotic. And like I said, it could have been anyone. I'm pretty sure it was more than two people, but it's hard to be certain. The walls may be thin, but they aren't that thin."

"You should call the station," the private detective told him. "Tell them what you remembered. Is there anything else? Any strange cars hanging around? Did anything unusual happen after the shooting?"

"No, no, nothing," Harrison said, shaking his head. "I'm sorry I can't be of more help."

"You've been plenty helpful," Moira assured him. "Thanks for your time." David reached into his pocket and took out a business card to hand to the old man.

"If you remember anything else, I'd appreciate if you gave me a call... right after you let the police know, of course," he told the man.

"I will. And good luck finding him. He was a good neighbor."

# CHAPTER TEN

None of the other neighbors answered their knocks, so Moira and David were forced to call their impromptu search to a close. The management office was empty and dark when they passed it on their way out of the complex, though David assured her that they would probably be reluctant to talk about one of their tenants anyway. She tried not to feel disappointed, but she had hoped to find more than just a grumpy neighbor to talk to. Where could Dante possibly be? Was he even still alive? She had been going on the assumption that the fact that his car was gone meant that he had taken it and fled, but she could be wrong. Maybe whoever had shot the other young man had stolen Dante's car too.

David took her back to the deli, where she bade him goodnight and got into her own car. It was full dark by then, and the town was almost eerily still. It seemed hard to imagine that her young employee could be out there alone and scared—or worse. She wished that there was more that she could do to find him, but she couldn't think of anything else that she could try. If he was still alive, he was on his own.

———

The next day, Friday, was supposed to be one of the rare days that neither Moira nor Candice worked at the deli, but with Dante missing, she knew that she would have to go in. Instead of canceling their plans to go back into Lake Marion and continue the search for the perfect store location for her daughter, she decided to wake up early and walk around Lake Marion before the deli opened.

"I know that you really like the toy store," she told Candice as they navigated the slippery roads between Maple Creek and Lake Marion. "But David still hasn't heard back from the owner, and he may end up not selling it. It would be great if you could find a place that you like almost as much in case the toy store falls through."

"I'll look," her daughter said doubtfully. "But it's not a huge town, and only a few buildings are up for rent." She sighed. "It's just that location is so important when it comes to having a successful business, and that place is perfect."

Moira smiled to herself, mentally comparing the difference between how her daughter was now and how she had been only a few short years ago. Even as a teenager, Candice had been relatively responsible. She had only really gotten in trouble twice that Moira could remember, and even those two incidents paled in comparison to some of those that she had heard about her friends' kids. Teenage Candice hadn't paid much attention to the future, and rarely took the time to talk to her mother; traits that seemed to have completely reversed after her daughter had come back from college. She often wondered what her life would be like without the young woman sitting in the car, and found it hard to imagine. Her daughter brought so much light and joy into her life that it was hard to think what it would be like without her.

"I'm sure you'll end up finding the right place," she reassured her daughter. "You've still got a while to look. Just take your time and don't rush things. You're welcome to stay at the house for as long as you want, you know."

"Oh man, that reminds me, I've got to find an apartment too. I don't want to have to make this drive every day." The young woman groaned. "There's so much that I have to do." Her mother chuckled.

"Welcome to adulthood," she said quietly, touching Candice's shoulder gently.

# CHAPTER ELEVEN

They got to town and decided to look at a building that had just gone up for rent. It was a bit farther from the intersection in the center of town than the toy store was, but it wasn't so far out that people would be unable to walk to it. It was currently serving as a small leather repair shop. Moira wandered towards the back, trying to envision shelves of candy lining the walls. It just didn't have the same feel that the toy store did. Her daughter was right; the toy store really was the perfect place for a candy shop.

"Mom, come here," came an urgent call from the front of the leather shop. She rushed over, wondering what could possibly have happened.

"What is it?" she asked when she reached her daughter. The young woman was standing at the front window, looking out onto Lake Marion's Main Street.

"I think... I think I just saw Dante's car," she said, keeping her eyes on the road as if expecting it to zip past again.

"Here? Really?" Moira joined her at the window. "Are you sure?"

"I'm not a hundred percent positive, but it definitely looked like it. It had that rusty patch on the door and everything."

"Which way did it go?"

Her daughter pointed to the left, and Moira gave the real estate agent who had been showing them the building a quick apology. With Candice following, she left the building and strode across the sidewalk to her car. As soon as they were both in with their seat belts on, she started the engine and took off down the road.

"Keep your eyes peeled, and look down side streets," she instructed her daughter. She kept her own eyes on the road and on the cars in front of her. She knew that she might be on a wild goose chase, but it felt good to be doing *something*.

"I don't see him," Candice said after they had been driving for a few minutes. "Maybe it wasn't even his car. I don't think we're going to find him like this."

"We can't just stop looking," she told her daughter. "He could be close. What if this is our only chance?"

"If he wanted us to find him, then he would just show up at the deli," her daughter pointed out. "We don't even know if he's alive, Mom. Even if it *was* his car that I saw, anyone could be driving it."

Gritting her teeth, Moira slowed down and turned into a gas station parking lot, using the space to turn her car around. Her daughter was right. It was doubtful that they would find him by driving around in circles like this. At best, it was a waste of gas, and at worse... well, she wouldn't want to end up like the guy who had been murdered.

They had just left town when her cell phone started buzzing in the drink holder between the front seats. She glanced at it and asked her daughter to see who it was.

"The caller ID says 'Jefferson,'" Candice told her. Feeling apprehensive, Moira took the phone from her and accepted the call. Whatever he wanted, it couldn't be good.

"Hello?" she said.

"Ms. Darling, are you all right?"

"Yes," she replied warily. "What's going on?"

"There's been an incident at your deli. I think you should get there as soon as possible."

"Is anyone hurt?" she asked, her heart pounding in her chest.

"No ma'am, at least, not that we've found."

"Okay." She took a deep breath to steady herself. "I'll be right there."

# CHAPTER TWELVE

David was sitting at his desk, looking over files and enjoying a late lunch of cold Italian food, when Moira called him. The grin that appeared on his face when he saw her caller ID faded quickly as she spoke.

"I'm on my way over," he promised. "You drive safely; don't rush." His pasta salad forgotten, the private detective shrugged into his coat, grabbed his keys, and headed for the parking lot.

The deli's parking lot looked crowded with three police cruisers and a fire truck sitting in it. He didn't see any smoke rising from the small building, for which he was grateful, but the shattered glass window in front was evident from the street. There was a huge fan blowing air out of the deli into the parking lot. David looked into the shop and noticed sparkling shards of glass littering the floor inside. Moira and Candice were standing in the parking lot next to the young detective who had spoken to them a few nights ago about Dante.

"David, I'm so glad you're here," Moira said when she saw him approaching. She looked pale and shaken. He didn't blame her. In fact, he felt pretty shaken himself when he thought about what might have happened if she had been in the deli when the break-in happened.

"Was anyone hurt?" he asked, giving her a quick hug without thinking about it. She stiffened for a moment, and then relaxed.

"No, thank goodness. Darrin wasn't here yet, and Candice and I were in Lake Marion looking at some leather place for her candy shop." Her green-eyed gaze drifted towards the deli. "Why would anyone do this?" He was surprised to see tears in her eyes; she had been through so much in the past few months and he'd never seen her cry. He realized that the deli must mean a lot to her.

"I don't know—do the police have any leads?" he asked, shooting a glance at Detective Jefferson, who shook his head.

"One of our patrol officers saw it while he was driving by," he explained to David. "We haven't been here for much longer than Ms. Darling has."

"We're right on Main Street," the private investigator responded angrily. "Are you telling me that no one else noticed this all morning? No one saw anything? It's a small town; everyone here knows Moira. Why wouldn't they report that her deli had been *broken into*?" Detective Jefferson just shrugged.

"That actually happens pretty often," he explained. "Everyone who saw the broken window just assumed either that someone else had already reported it or that Moira already knew. It's in such a public place that they probably didn't think there would even be a point in reporting it."

"And you have no idea who did it?" David asked.

"I gave them a copy of the recording from the camera," Moira cut in, referencing the video camera that he had installed for her a few weeks ago. "Its lens captures most of the front window; we should get a clear shot of whoever broke in easily enough."

"That's good, at least." He frowned, gazing across the parking lot. "Why is there a fire truck here? Did someone set a fire?"

"Not a fire, no," she replied. Hesitating, she chewed her lip. "But, well, whoever broke in *did* turn all of the gas burners onto high. Who knows what would have happened if a spark had somehow gone off in there before it was aired out."

"Wow," David said, stunned. "I'm just glad you're all right."

"I think we have everything we need here, ma'am," Jefferson cut in. "We'll get out of your hair. Feel free to start cleaning up as soon as the fire department gives you the all clear. We'll let you know as soon as we catch the person that did this." Moira responded to the detective with a distracted goodbye. After two firefighters carrying fans came out of the deli and told her it was safe, she turned back to David.

"I need to call my insurance agent," she told him, staring past him at the broken window with shock still in her eyes. "I already called Darrin. He should be here soon."

"I'll stay and help," he told her. "Just tell me what you need me to do."

"I don't even know where to begin," she admitted in a quiet, defeated voice. "The entire place is ransacked. I'm going to need to throw most of the food out, and one of the walls needs repainting... not to mention the window, of course. I think my insurance covers it, but I'm not positive."

"Let's start by cleaning up the glass," he said gently. "You handle the call to the insurance. I know where everything is." She gave him a pale imitation of her usual bright smile and pulled her cell phone out of her pocket.

David turned his attention to the shattered window and was glad he was wearing his sturdy winter boots. Only a few jagged shards remained in the large window frame. The rest of the glass was scattered around the floor of the deli. Some pieces were as long as his forearm, but most were much smaller.

He hoped that the insurance would end up covering most of the repair costs. He didn't even want to think how much it would cost out of pocket to repair a window that size. Once he found whoever did this to Moira's cherished store, he would do his best to make sure they spent as long as possible behind bars.

# CHAPTER THIRTEEN

Moira put her phone back in her pocket, feeling much better after having spoken to her insurance agent. She had been assured that she would only have to pay a deductible and the insurance company would cover the rest of the cost of replacing the window. At least she wouldn't have to use the money that she had set aside to help Candice open her candy shop, which had been one of her primary concerns.

She joined David inside, where he was staring at the wall to the right of the register, an unreadable expression on his face. Scrawled on the wall in permanent marker was a demand from whoever had broken in. *Give him up, or your next.* The threat put shivers down her spine. This hadn't been some random robbery—in fact, nothing seemed to be missing at all, so it couldn't properly be called a robbery. No, this was personal. Someone had targeted her specifically, trying to scare her into doing something. The only problem was, she didn't know what it was that they wanted.

"What did the police think of this?" the private investigator asked.

"I don't know. They took pictures—a lot of pictures—but they didn't really say much." She frowned, staring at the words. "Any idea what it could mean?"

"My guess is someone thinks you know where Dante is," he replied. Moira gaped at him. Of course; it made perfect sense now that he said it. Who else would someone be looking for?

"But I don't know where Dante is," she pointed out.

"I haven't heard from him since..." she trailed off, remembering her and Candice's impromptu search for the young man in Lake Marion earlier. She had forgotten it with all the excitement.

"What?" David said, giving her a sharp look.

"It's just that Candice said she thought she saw his car when we were in Lake Marion this morning. We drove around and tried to see if we could find him, but we didn't have any luck. Do you think whoever is looking for him knows that he's still around?"

"Likely," he said. "But if you really haven't seen him, then why would this person think you know where he is?"

"Because according to everyone we've spoken to, Candice, Darrin, and I were the only locals Dante really knew," she pointed out. A moment later she added, "Even if I *did* know where he is though, I wouldn't betray him just because someone trashed the deli."

"I know." David gave her fond look. "You're one of the most loyal people I know, Moira."

The sound of a car pulling into the lot made Mora look away from the private investigator. It was Darrin, pulling up in his truck. She saw his eyes widen as he got out of the truck and got a good look at the place where the window had been. He gave a low whistle.

"Wow, someone really has it in for you, Ms. D.," he said. "A dead guy found in the deli during the Winter Festival, and now this?"

"It's not as bad as it looks," she said weakly. "The insurance covers most of it. It could have been a lot worse."

"That's true. How's the rest of the place?" He stepped through the door, which had been propped open to let the police in and out easily. He paled when he read the words on the wall.

"Whoever did this took most of the stuff out of the fridges and the freezer," she told him. "They also left all of the gas appliances on high, but the fire marshal took care of that. Other than the window and the wall, it will mostly be a lot of cleaning. You should have seen the floor in here before David started to clear out some of the glass." The private investigator had swept most of the glass into paper bags, and had knocked out the deadly looking shards left in the window.

"Who would do this?" Darrin asked, shaking his head in disbelief. "What would have happened if one of us had been here?"

"I don't even want to think about that," Moira replied with a shudder. "Let's just start cleaning. Candice is picking up some new paint for the wall. You and I can get started on taking care of the food."

It took them a few hours, but eventually they got Darling's DELIcious Delights back into an acceptable state. She had been devastated to find that only about half the food had been salvageable, but felt lucky the loss of food was the worst of the damage, besides the window. David had done a good job clearing up the broken glass, and except for the missing window, the front room looked almost normal thanks to Candice's quick paint job. She was grateful that whoever had vandalized the place had left the expensive refrigerated glass display cases intact. She would likely be able to open the deli normally tomorrow, once she had gotten a sheet or tarp to cover the window frame.

"What did the camera catch?" David asked with a nod at the security camera above the register.

"It recorded the guy breaking the window and

writing on the wall, but nothing in the back," she said. "The recording isn't very helpful, though. He was wearing a ski-mask and a big coat the whole time."

"The motion detector in the back didn't go off?"

"I, um, forgot to reset it when I left last night," she admitted. "I won't be making that mistake again."

"That's too bad, but it can't be helped now," he said with a sigh. "Mind if I take a look at the footage from the break-in?"

Moira got her tablet out and sat at one of the small bistro tables with Darrin, Candice, and David huddled around her. She could access the security camera footage wirelessly through her cell phone or tablet, which was very convenient. The police had been emailed a copy of the footage as well, and she was sure that they would have some sort of expert analyzing it. All she had were the eyes of everyone at the table with her; that would have to suffice.

She started the video a few seconds before the masked figure smashed the window in with a brick. The violence was astounding; it was obvious that he had meant to do serious damage to the deli, not just to find a way in. She almost wished that he had been a simple burglar. This spiteful vandalism was more frightening.

The figure in the video was tall, but every inch of his skin was covered. She was pretty certain that the criminal was a man; something about the way he moved just seemed masculine to her. He wrote the threatening message on the wall, then spent only a few minutes in the back, to dump large amounts of expensive food on the floor and to turn on the gas burners on the stove, before running back through the front room and leaving.

"Feel free to play it again if you want to," the deli

owner told the private investigator. "I've already watched it a few times though, and I can't see a single clue as to who it could be."

"I'll watch it again later, if you'll send me a copy of the file," he told her. "I think I'll be able to see it better on my computer. There wasn't anything else abnormal from last night? Did you watch the footage from yesterday to see if anyone of a similar build came in?"

"I skimmed through it," Moira said. "Plus, the police have it. Maybe I should also watch some of the other days from this week. That guy was pretty tall, I'm sure he'd stand out in the footage even with other people around."

"It's a good idea. You can never be too thorough." He frowned. "What day did Dante disappear? Can you watch the footage from that night?"

She did as he suggested, fast-forwarding the footage of the dark deli until a shadowy form appeared on screen. Moira paused the video and zoomed in on the person's face. When she saw who it was, she gasped.

CHAPTER FOURTEEN

"It's Dante," she said.

"You don't think he's the one that broke in, do you?"
Candice asked, leaning forward to get a better look
at the paused video on her mother's tablet.

"Whoever broke in was much taller than Dante,"
David pointed out. "But my question is, what is he
doing in the deli the night of the murder? He would
have already been on the run, wouldn't he?"

"This is about six hours after we got the call to go

and identify the body," Moira told him. "So yes, he would have already been on the run."

"Do you think he stole something?" Darrin asked. "Not, like, to be a jerk, but because he needed food or money and didn't want to use his credit card?"

"I didn't notice anything missing," the deli owner said. "And I'm pretty sure that I had remembered to set the motion detector that night, so I would have been alerted if he went in the back."

"He has to know about the camera." Her daughter glanced up at the security camera that was constantly recording everything that happened in the front room of the deli. "It took us all a while to get used to it, and you showed each of us what parts of the deli it can record from up there. If he had wanted to be sneaky, he wouldn't have walked right up to it."

"Play the video," David said. "Let's see what he does."

They watched as the young man walked past the camera towards the analog clock on the wall. He reached up, took down the clock, tucked something into the battery cover, and then put it back on the wall. On his return trip, he stopped right beneath the camera and looked up at it with an unreadable expression on his face. Then he left, locking the deli's front door carefully behind him.

The four of them traded a glance, and then David strode over to the clock and took it down. After a moment of fumbling, he withdrew a folded slip of paper from the back of it, which he brought over to Moira.

"It's a note," he said. She took it and unfolded it, her heart pounding.

*Dear Ms. D., I hope you find this. I just wanted to let you know that I'm okay, and I didn't kill anybody. I can't tell you where I am or what's going on in case the person who's after me finds this, but I didn't want everyone at the deli to think I'm a murderer. I hope none of this affects you, and I'm really sorry if I've caused you trouble. -D*

She handed it off to Candice once she had finished reading it, and then looked up at David.

"He didn't do it," she said with relief. David nodded.

"He could be lying, but I don't think so." He frowned, glancing down at the note once more. "I just wish he had given us more to go on. How are we supposed to help him if we don't know how to contact him?"

"We still don't know who the killer is either," Moira pointed out. "It could be anyone. I might see them every day, or they might be a complete stranger."

"Just be careful, and don't go anywhere alone," he told her. "You said you saw Dante in Lake Marion last?"

"I think so," Candice told him. "Well, I saw his car at least."

"All right, I'm going to go take a look around. I'll take another look at the footage from last night, too." He looked at each of them in turn. "You three be careful. We still don't know exactly what's going on, and if someone thinks one of you is helping Dante, you all could be in danger."

"We'll be careful," the deli owner promised. "I should probably call Detective Jefferson and tell him about the note. You be careful too, David. If the killer is targeting people that Dante knows, you could be a target as well. You've known him for as long as I have."

The private investigator gave a brief nod, and then bid her and her employees a farewell. Moira could tell by the look in his eyes that he was eager to get to work. Despite everything, she felt a small smile tug at the corners of her mouth. They really weren't that different from each other—they both loved a mystery, after all.

There was no way that they would be able to officially open the deli today, so Moira sent Darrin home and started working on order forms to replace the food that had been destroyed. Some items would be harder to replace than others, since most fresh produce wasn't in season right now. They would scrape by, though. She was already trying to figure out how much they would have to change the specials that she had planned out for the next week. At least she had the freedom to tweak the recipes if she had to.

She was just putting the order forms in her purse when her cell phone began to buzz. A glance at the screen told her that it was Detective Jefferson for the second time that day. *What could it possibly be now?* she wondered.

"Ms. Darling, do you think you could meet me at your house? There was another attempted break-in," he said.

"Wait, hold on," she said, her mind whirling. "Someone tried to break into my house?"

"Yes ma'am. And this time, we caught them in the act."

# CHAPTER FIFTEEN

After locking up the deli as best she could—anyone would be able to get in through the open window, after all—she and Candice hurried back to the house. A single patrol vehicle was waiting for them, out of which Detective Jefferson stepped when they pulled into the driveway.

"It's been a rough day, I know," he said when they got out of the car. "This shouldn't take long."

"Is the house all right?" Moira asked, half expecting to see another broken window.

"The back door is slightly scratched where the perp tried to force it open with a crowbar, but luckily one of our officers stopped him before any real damage could be done," he told her.

"Did you arrest him?" she asked.

"Sadly, he got away. But I think it was the same guy. He was wearing an outfit similar to what the person in the video was wearing, and left the same shoe prints in the snow."

"Thank goodness my daughter and I weren't here this time either," Moira said. "Did someone report him? How did you see him if he was in the back?"

"I sent a squad car over to keep an eye on your place," the detective said with a shrug. "It was just a hunch, but it turned out to be a good one. The note left on the wall at the deli made it clear that someone was targeting you specifically."

"Well, I'm glad you did. Thanks. I don't think I could stand another mess like the one at the deli." She sighed, feeling tired and angry at whoever was making life miserable for her and her employees. "What do you need me to do?"

After Moira took a quick peek inside and walked around the outside of her house with the officer to make sure nothing was damaged or missing, Jefferson seemed satisfied that she and Candice would be safe there alone. Moira remembered the note right before he left, and handed it to him with a quick explanation of how they had found it. After promising to email him the video footage from that night too, she and her daughter thanked him one last time and watched him drive away.

***

After getting off the phone with Moira, David sat in silence for a few moments. He couldn't understand what it was about the deli owner that seemed to attract so much trouble. She was honest and kind-hearted; in no way did she deserve all that had been happening to her. He was just glad that her house hadn't been ransacked—it had been good thinking on the part of Detective Jefferson to send a squad car out to keep an eye on things. He hoped that someone would be watching her house tonight, too, in case the masked vandal decided to try again.

The question was, had the person been looking for something in particular, or was he just there to cause chaos? David had the gut feeling that whoever it was thought that Moira was hiding Dante in her house. The need to find the young man was getting more and more urgent. Innocent or not, the longer Dante was gone, the longer Moira's life would be in danger. Watching the video of the deli break-in again and again wasn't going to help—he needed to get out there and find the missing employee.

He decided that his best bet would be to get organized first. There would be no use just driving around and hoping that he happened to cross paths with Dante, especially not with dusk falling. No, in the morning he would start at one end of town and work his way through, checking at each hotel, motel, and rest stop. If he didn't find the kid in Lake Marion, he would head to Maple Creek and start looking there. *Someone* thought that Dante was still in town, and as long as they thought that, Moira and the people she cared about would be in danger.

# CHAPTER SIXTEEN

Armed with a hot thermos of coffee and a picture of Dante's car, David set out early the next morning to see if he could find the missing deli employee. At first, he was optimistic, but as the hours passed and he didn't see any sign of the vehicle, he began to lose hope. There was no proof that Dante was even still *around*. For all David knew, the young man could be halfway to Oklahoma. Even if Candice had seen his car the day before, the kid could still be long gone. The search was beginning to feel more and more like a wild goose chase.

He was on the verge of giving up when he hit pay dirt. A car that perfectly matched the one in the picture had just crossed through an intersection in front of him—complete with the spot of rust on the door. Feeling adrenaline flood his veins, he forced himself not to accelerate and instead took the turn at a normal speed. Keeping far enough back that the driver of the car in front of him wouldn't realize that he was being followed, David tailed him.

The car led him on a slow tour through town, and eventually ended up on one of the long, curving highways that would eventually come to the coast of Lake Michigan. The lake was a good half hour away, and it looked like the car was going to putter along the whole way there. Trying to force himself to stay back, remain calm, and focus on not spooking Dante, David settled in for the ride.

Just a few miles before the rolling hills and sandy woods gave way to the beach, the car turned off at an unmarked intersection that David had probably driven past a hundred times before without noticing. He slowed his car and paused for a moment before turning; on such a small road, it would be obvious that he was following the other car. He was reluctant to give up his advantage of surprise, but didn't want to risk losing the vehicle. He would just have to hope that he had indeed been following the right car, and that Dante wasn't too jumpy.

The dirt road was bumpy and rough, with dry dirt giving way to sudden pits of sand that threatened to bog down his vehicle. The half-melted ice just served to make everything even more slippery, and David had to concentrate just to keep his car on the track. Dante's car had disappeared around a curve, and he was worried for a second that he had lost it. When he rounded the corner, however, he saw that it had pulled off to the side, and the driver's side door was open. *This could get interesting,* he thought as he pulled up behind the car. He glanced in the windows as he walked up to make sure no one was in it, and then turned towards the trees.

"Dante," he called out. "It's David Morris, Moira Darling's friend. I want to help." He waited, tense, knowing that so much could go wrong. Relief flowed through his when a slim form appeared from behind an old tree.

"You shouldn't have followed me," Dante said. "You don't know what's going on—you could get hurt."

"I think you need to start at the beginning," the private detective told him. "And tell me everything. I can help... and if I can't, I can get you to someone who can."

He listened to the young man's story with growing concern. It sounded like the person they were dealing with had a lot of blood on his hands already, and wouldn't hesitate to shed some more. Wondering once again how Moira managed to find such trouble seemingly out of nowhere, David ushered Dante into his car.

"Come with me," he said. "We'll stop by the deli and tell Moira what's going on, and then get you to the police station. Tell them what you just told me, and don't hold anything back."

# CHAPTER SEVENTEEN

Thanks to the helpful man from the local hardware shop, Moira got to the deli in the morning to discover that a bundle of plastic sheeting had been donated to temporarily cover the gaping hole where the window had been while she waited for the repair company to come out and fix it. It was a simple matter for her and Candice to tape it up. The plastic served better as windbreak than insulation, but at least she no longer had to worry about snow blowing in.

She got started on the soup of the day as soon as the plastic was up, and sent her daughter to town to pick up some necessities from the grocery store. With slices of pork sizzling away in a pan with onions and carrots, and the potatoes slowly coming to a boil, she was feeling much better. It was good to be back in the usual rhythm of things. She just had to keep telling herself that Dante would be okay, and that all of this would get solved before she knew it.

She didn't know what to expect at the deli that day. By now, surely the whole town had either heard about the break-in, or seen the shattered window as they drove past. There would likely be a lot of sight-seers, so she decided to make extra soup. The creamy pork and potato soup was rich and filling, with just a hint of clove. It was a new recipe, and the best she could do with her limited ingredients. She hoped that the delicious smell would entice the curious townsfolk who stopped by to buy a bowl before they left. With all of the goods that she had to replace, she could certainly use the money.

Once the deli had officially opened for the day, she found herself busy enough not to dwell on any of her concerns. The townspeople—her regulars— were all concerned and supportive. A couple of people suggested that she set up some sort of donation jar to help with the money that she would need to replace the destroyed food and pay off the insurance deductible for the window, but she declined, not liking the thought of taking donated money for business expenses.

During a rare break in the rush of people, she sent Candice to the back to start on some of the dishes while she took the opportunity to call the local window shop and see how long it would take them to do a custom double pane of glass for her. A customer walked in while she was on hold, and she glanced up to mouth a quick *I'm sorry* to him. Then she did a double take, something about the tall man standing in front of her nudging her memory.

He was thin, with blonde hair, and looked familiar. Where had she seen him before? She wasn't sure, but she thought that he had come in the day before Dante had disappeared. She remembered her employee's odd reaction when he saw him, and her decision not to question him about it. Now she really wished that she had.

With her pulse pounding in her ears, she hung up on the window repair company and slowly turned away from him. All she could think of was to get Candice and get out. If this was the man that Dante had been afraid of, and the same one who had ransacked the deli, then she and her daughter were in danger.

She hadn't gone more than a few steps before she heard movement behind her. She didn't even have time to spin around before a hand pressed a sweet, almost rotten-smelling cloth against her mouth and nose. Struggling, she tried not to breathe it in, but to no avail. After only a few seconds, she was getting dizzy. It felt like someone had stuffed cotton into her ears, and her vision was going blurry. She hardly even noticed it as he dragged her out the front door and shoved her into a car. Her head hit the roof, and everything went black.

## CHAPTER EIGHTEEN

"Are you finally waking up?"

Still feeling disoriented, Moira did her best to sit up. Her head was aching, both from where she had hit it on the car, and a duller, more insidious ache that was probably from whatever sickeningly sweet chemical had been on the cloth. The last few minutes—or had it been longer?—were just a disoriented jumble of memories to her. As if to add insult to injury, her stomach suddenly clenched with nausea. Biting the inside of her cheek in hopes that the pain would help her get back to normal quickly, she tried not to vomit as she looked around.

She was in a car parked in what looked like a camp-ground. The lot was empty except for an ancient mobile home and a charcoal grill. The car smelled bad, like old shoes and stale cigar smoke. There were fast food wrappers crumpled to the floor. The tall man who was sitting in the driver's seat nudged her.

"Get up already. I've been waiting around too long. Shouldn't have hit your head; I think that knocked you out more than the chloroform did."

"What... what's going on?" she asked. She made the mistake of moving her head to allow her a better look at him, and the world spun.

"I got fed up with waiting. I need to find the kid, and you're going to help. Come on." He got out of the car and walked over to open her door, grabbing her and pulling her out of the vehicle by force. She tumbled unceremoniously to the ground, trying—and failing—to catch herself.

"I don't know where he is," she mumbled as she struggled to her feet. Her eyes darted to the forest that seemed to press in from all sides. Should she run? No... she could barely stand, and she knew her unsteady stomach would foil any escape attempt. Maybe he would let her just stand here and lean against the car for a while. No such luck.

"Don't lie to me." He grabbed her by the arm and yanked her towards the mobile home. "One of you has got to be hiding him. If it's not you, then who is it? That blonde girl? The other guy that works at the deli? How about the private eye? One of them knows where the kid is; he doesn't know anyone else here."

"None of us have seen him, I promise," Moira managed to gasp out. Her nausea was only increasing, but she didn't want to risk making the man even more angry by vomiting. "Who are you? Why are you after Dante?"

"Let's just say it's a personal grudge. I spent eleven years in prison thanks to him," the man sneered. "And his little traitor cousin thought he could warn him. I showed him though, didn't I?"

He seemed to be talking to himself when he said this. He was staring off into space, his eyes wild and bloodshot, as if he was reliving the past all over again in that moment. Moira tripped, falling to her knees in the snow. Her arm was yanked out of her assailant's grasp, but he didn't seem to care.

"Even if you don't know where the kid is hiding, you'll still help me," he was saying. "You can be another message for him, how would you like that? Maybe he'll come out of hiding once I start killing his friends one by one."

As her mind became clearer and the remnants of the chloroform's chemical anesthesia faded, panic began to set in. The man seemed beyond reason. He was obviously off his rocker, and had proven himself to be dangerous. And while she was thinking more clearly now, her head was still pounding and she didn't know whether she would be able to stand. Running still seemed out of the question. Even if she could make it to the trees, where would she go? They were probably a few miles outside of town, and she didn't even have her coat on. Her cell phone must have been dropped when the man attacked her, and she was definitely not in any state to try to find her way back to civilization on her own.

Thinking of her cell phone brought her to her daughter and the fact that Candice had likely walked out of the back room to find her mother gone, having left behind her phone and car. What must she have thought? Hopefully Candice had noticed Moira's absence quickly and had called the cops as soon as she could. She would just have to hope that someone was looking for her and fall back on her tried and true practice of stalling for as long as she could.

"What makes you think Dante is even still around?"

she asked. "Wouldn't it be smarter for him to have left town as soon as he knew you were looking for him?"

"I saw his car a couple of times," the man grunted. "Always while I was on foot, though. Oh, he's around. He's watching me. He has nowhere else to go, and he knows it. This is the end of the line."

"You said you were in prison," Moira began, casting about for anything that she could think of to try to change his mind. "It must have been horrible there. Is revenge really worth the risk of going back?"

"I got a one-way ticket to Mexico, sweets," he told her with a dry laugh. "Just gotta finish up my business here first. Once he's taken care of, I'm not gonna be sticking around to see what happens next, if you get my drift." He frowned down at her, as if just suddenly realizing that she had fallen.

"Get up and go inside unless you want me to shoot you right here. I'm cold, I need a good warm coffee." He reached for her and she shrank back, certain that if he got her inside the mobile home, she wouldn't be coming back out. Fear gave her strength, and she struggled to her feet, ignoring the way that the world seemed to spin around her head. Some part of her realized faintly that she could have a concussion. He had slammed her head against the car pretty hard. It looked like she was going to have to make a break for it. At least even if he did catch her, she would have tried to escape. Taking a deep breath, she did her best to push her throbbing head and the insistent nausea out of her mind. It was time to make her move.

# CHAPTER NINETEEN

It seemed like once she made her decision, every-thing happened at once. The man lunged at her, and she took off, stumbling and weaving her way across the snow-covered grass. She stumbled twice, but managed to keep her feet under her and keep going. Her kidnapper was hot on her heels, and already she could feel a stitch in her side. She wouldn't be able to keep this up for long.

Suddenly, just as he was closing in on her, a familiar black car burst out of the trees. It skidded along the path, coming to a stop just behind the kidnapper's vehicle. She changed course, heading back towards the cars, and heard her kidnapper swear behind her.

Moments later, he bowled into her, sending her crashing down to the ground. She kicked out at him, but missed. Her second kick connected with his shoulder, but she couldn't put enough force behind it to hurt him. He seemed determined to finish what he had started, even though her rescuers were only moments away and were running to save her.

Luckily he either didn't have a weapon, or hadn't thought to get it out. He clawed at her, struggling to try to reach her throat, but she was able to get her feet up and kick him away. If he'd had a knife or a gun out, she would be dead by now, and she was very aware of that fact.

After what seemed like an eternity but was really only a few seconds, David and Dante reached them. The private detective grabbed the blond man by his shoulders and yanked him off of her. All of the fight seemed to go out of him for a moment until he saw Dante, and then his face twisted into a vicious expression of hatred and anger. David seemed to expect it, and instead of trying to hold him back, he shoved him forward so that the man did a face plant in the snow. In a flash, he handcuffed him and pocketed the key. Then he turned to Moira and helped her up, wrapping her in a warm hug as soon as he saw that she wasn't seriously hurt.

"You found Dante," she said once he had released her. "How did you know I was here?"

"My cousin told me Stephan was staying at a campsite near town," Dante said. "That's what I've been doing these last few days. Looking for him. This was the only campsite I hadn't checked yet."

"We took a chance," David told her. "While the police were doing things the slow way, we came here."

"I'm glad you did," Moira said. "Tell me everything. Why was this guy after him? Why did he kill his cousin? What's going on?"

"Later," David said. "First, we've got to take Stephan to the police station and get your employee's name cleared. Everything else can wait."

———————

It took them hours to explain everything to the police. The three of them had a separate portion of the story to tell and they were questioned separately. At first it seemed like Dante would have to stay behind bars at least for the night until they could get a lawyer to figure things out. Somehow—by that point, Moira was beyond exhausted and was still battling a headache—David managed to convince the police that he would watch Dante and bring him back in the morning. By the time they left the station it was late, but she didn't want to go home without hearing the full story. Since David and Dante both seemed to be willing, she called up Candice and Darrin and asked them to meet her at the deli.

Once she had made five cups of coffee and Darrin

had dragged an old space heater out of the back to make the chilly front room bearable, she turned to Dante, who was looking at the broken window with a guilty expression.

"I'm glad you're okay," she began.

"Thanks. I'm glad you are too. I never wanted any of you to get hurt."

"I know. And I know you're probably exhausted... but I think we all need to hear at least the gist of what happened. How about you start with the guy that kidnapped me?"

"That was Stephan," he said. "It's a long story... but the short version is that some of my family—my aunt and uncle—got in over their heads with some really bad guys. I was pretty young when it happened, but I know that there was a lot of money involved, and drugs." He paused, taking a sip of his coffee and closing his eyes as he remembered. "I guess my aunt and uncle owed the drug dealers some pretty significant funds and tried to back out. As punishment, this gang sent someone to punish them. Since dead men don't pay, instead of killing my uncle and my aunt, he targeted their family—my parents. I watched them get killed when I was ten."

Candice and Darrin looked shocked and Moira said, "Oh, I'm so sorry, Dante,. You don't have to go on if you don't want to."

"No, I should," he said. "I think it's good to talk about it after not telling anyone for so long." He took a deep breath. "Obviously, the cops showed up, and a lot of confusing stuff happened. I ended up testifying in court, and I managed to identify the man who killed my parents. He made some sort of plea bargain—in exchange for giving up the other people in his gang, he got a shorter sentence. After that, I went into foster care and ended up moving a few towns away."

"How did you end up here?" she asked. "And how did you manage to fudge the background checks? David found out that you used to have a different last name."

"Oh, that." He gave a slightly embarrassed grimace. "Well, once I heard that Stephan was getting out of prison soon, I took my life savings and got a fake ID —nothing fancy, it was probably a really terrible job in fact. The guy I went to was pretty shady. I just wanted to make it harder for Stephan to track me down. I had a feeling he'd be pretty mad at me for getting him sent to prison, so I ran. I came here because my parents had once rented a cabin in the area when I was younger, and I liked it. I probably should have chosen somewhere I'd never been to, but I fell in love with this place."

"Why didn't you go to the police?" David asked. "And how was your cousin involved in all of this?"

"I guess my cousin sort of got sucked into the same

sort of life that my aunt and uncle lived," Dante said. "I never really heard from him much until he showed up at my door in a panic, telling me to run because Stephan was coming to kill me. A moment later Stephan himself showed up. He called my cousin a traitor and shot him. I was lucky to escape. And as for the police..." He shrugged. "That's not how I grew up. For my family, the police were the bad guys."

"I hope you don't think that anymore," the private investigator said.

"No sir, I don't," her employee replied. "I'm just grateful that they gave me a chance to tell my story."

"Thanks for repeating it to us," Moira said, offering him a gentle smile. "I know it couldn't have been easy."

"Thanks for giving me a chance, Ms. D." He stood up

and looked around at the deli. "I'll miss this place, and I'll miss all of you guys."

"What are you talking about?" she asked with a frown.

"Well, I'm fired, aren't I?" he said. "Because of me, the deli got broken into and you got attacked."

"Of course you're not fired. Right, Mom?" Candice interjected.

"Of course not," Moira said firmly. "This is your home. And now that Stephan is behind bars—this time for good—hopefully you'll be able to have a normal life here."

Darrin, Candice, and David all raised their voices, talking over one another to convince Dante to stay. The deli owner smiled to herself as she watched them. They all had their own troubles and busy lives but when it was important, they always managed to be there for each other. She couldn't imagine a better set of friends to have.

Book 33: Murder, My Darling

**Killer Cookie Series**

Book 1: Killer Caramel Cookies

Book 2: Killer Halloween Cookies

Book 3: Killer Maple Cookies

Book 4: Crunchy Christmas Murder

Book 5: Killer Valentine Cookies

**Asheville Meadows Series**

Book 1: Small Town Murder

Book 2: Murder on Aisle Three

Book 3: The Heart of Murder

Book 4: Dating is Murder

Book 5: Dying to Cook

Book 6: Food, Family and Murder

Book 7: Fish, Chips and Murder

**Cozy Mystery Tails of Alaska**

Book 1: Mushing is Murder

Book 2: Murder Befalls Us

Book 3: Stage Fright and Murder

Book 4: Routine Murder

Book 5: Best Friends and Betrayal

Book 6: Tick Tock and Treachery

## AUTHOR'S NOTE

I'd love to hear your thoughts on my books, the storylines, and anything else that you'd like to comment on—reader feedback is very important to me. My contact information, along with some other helpful links, is listed on the next page. If you'd like to be on my list of "folks to contact" with updates, release and sales notifications, etc.... just shoot me an email and let me know. Thanks for reading!

Also...

... if you're looking for more great reads, Summer Prescott Books publishes several popular series by outstanding Cozy Mystery authors.

# CONTACT SUMMER PRESCOTT BOOKS PUBLISHING

Twitter: @summerprescott1

Bookbub:

https://www.bookbub.com/authors/summer-prescott

Blog and Book Catalog:
http://summerprescottbooks.com

Email: summer.prescott.cozies@gmail.com

YouTube:
https://www.youtube.com/channel/UCngKNUkDd
WuQ5k7-Vkfrp6A

And...be sure to check out the Summer Prescott Cozy Mysteries fan page and Summer Prescott Books Publishing Page on Facebook – let's be friends!

To download a free book, and sign up for our fun and exciting newsletter, which will give you opportunities to win prizes and swag, enter contests, and be the first to know about New Releases, click here: http://summerprescottbooks.com

CPSIA information can be obtained
at www.ICGtesting.com
Printed in the USA
LVHW081421140520
655613LV00018B/1624